S0-BDL-363

Our Veronica

goes to Petunia's farm

written and illustrated by

ROGER DUVOISIN

Alfred A. Knopf  New York

TO MICHEL

L. C. Catalog card number: 62–14767

THIS IS A BORZOI BOOK, PUBLISHED BY ALFRED A. KNOPF, INC.

Copyright © 1962 by Roger Duvoisin
All rights reserved. No part of this book may be reproduced in any form without permission in writing from the publisher, except by a reviewer, who may quote brief passages and reproduce not more than three illustrations in a review to be printed in a magazine or newspaper. Manufactured in the United States of America, and distributed by Random House, Inc. Published simultaneously in Toronto, Canada, by Random House of Canada, Ltd.

It was on a sunny morning that Veronica arrived at Mr. Pumpkin's farm. At once she saw it was a lovely place. Just right for a hippopotamus.

There was a little pond to splash and turn somersaults in—just the right size for one hippopotamus.

There was a mud puddle at the end of the pond—just the right mud for wallowing.

There was a beautiful meadow—just the right grass for eating.

And there were many animals to gossip with: Petunia the goose, Straw the horse, Cotton the cat, Clover the cow, Noisy the dog, Charles the gander, Ida the hen, King the rooster, and Donkey, Goat, Sheep, Pig, Piggy, Duck, and others.

Truly, thought Veronica, a hippopotamus's paradise.

Veronica walked down the driveway to her new house. All the animals watched her from behind the barn. They did not know what to think.

"Woof, woof," barked Noisy the dog furiously, from behind Clover the cow. "What's that? Woof, woof, woof, woof!"

"I hope it does not bite," said Cotton the cat. "Its mouth is large enough to swallow Pig at one gulp."

"It's a hippopotamus," said Straw the horse. "I once saw a picture of one on a poster in town."

"Is that a new kind of farm animal?" asked Clover.

"Hippopotamuses come from circuses," said Straw. "I know that much."

"Well," said Ida the hen, "I don't like the look of a hippopotamus. It's neither a hen, nor a duck, nor a cow, nor a sheep, pig, donkey, goat, goose, horse, cat, dog. It has no place on a farm."

"We agree," said all the others.

The next day, when Veronica came out of her house, she greeted her new friends with a "GOOD MORNING" and a smile as big as her mouth.

They only grumbled: "Mmmm . . ." and did not even look at her.

"Good morning," repeated Veronica. "I am Veronica the hippopotamus."

"Mmmm . . ." said the farm animals again.

"I wonder what ails these people," thought Veronica. "I suppose they just have farm manners."

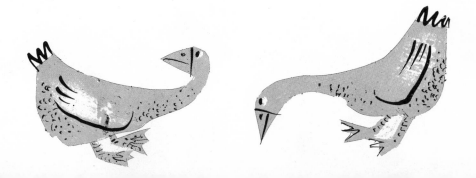

Veronica went all alone to the pond to bathe and splash. But, somehow, the pond did not seem as lovely today. It was no longer just right.

Veronica ate the grass with little appetite. It did not seem just right either. Even the mud puddle was no longer a just-right mud puddle.

Meanwhile, at the other end of the meadow, Ida the hen said: "Did you hear that loud 'GOOD MORNING'? IT thought we were friends. How arrogant."

"See how IT muddies the pond," said Clover. "We can't possibly drink that muddy water."

"And see how ITS big feet trample the grass," said Straw. "We can't possibly eat trampled grass."

"How ugly it is!"
said Pig.
        "Even the name is
ugly," said Cotton.

"Not a farm
name," said Goat. "A
zoo name. That's what
it is."

"Therefore
a foreigner," said
Donkey.

Every day, the farm animals stayed at the other end of the meadow.
They never said a word to Veronica.
Not even "good morning." Not even "good night."

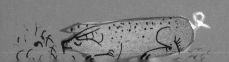

And every day, Veronica found the little pond less beautiful. The water was less refreshing. The green grass was less tasty.

She lost her fine, big appetite.

Then, one day, Veronica did not come out of her house.

Not for the whole day.

Nor the next day.

Not for *the whole week*.

"I wonder why IT stays in its house," said Straw one morning at the end of the week.

"Do you know what I think?" said Petunia. "I think IT does not look well."

"How do you know?" asked Noisy.

"Oh . . . I peeped through a crack in the door," answered Petunia.

"Ah . . . I peeped too," said Ida.

When Clover came into the pasture the next day she said: "It's true. IT is not well. IT is pale. And thin all over."

"How do *you* know?" asked Straw.

"Well . . . I pushed the window open and looked in."

"I *went* in," said Cotton, "through the cat's hole. IT *is* sick. It was just lying in the straw."

"*I* went in too," said King the rooster. "IT is *very* sick. It never even opened one eye. It does not eat."

"Do you think it will die?" asked Straw.

They all shook their heads sadly. Each one slowly wandered off to different parts of the farm. And so the day passed.

When they met in the meadow the next morning, Straw said:

"Do you know that VERONICA said 'thank you' this morning?"
"Why did she say 'thank you'?" asked Goat.
"Ah . . . well, I took some hay to her. Maybe she will eat it."

"And I gave her some
grain," said King. "All corn."

"And I gave her some mash," said Ida. "Egg-laying mash . . . the very best."

"And I gave her some dog food," said Noisy. "With gravy."

"And I gave her some potatoes," said Pig, "well rotten and tasty."

The next day it was Donkey who was first in the pasture. He rolled on his back, and brayed, and looked foolish.

"What's wrong with you?" asked Goat.

"Nothing. A nice morning. That's all. Oh . . . I took some thistle to Veronica and I said, 'Good morning.' And do you know what happened? She opened one eye and she said 'Good morning,' too."

"And do you know what else?" said Petunia and Charles the gander, wandering up. "We gave her our ration of bread soaked in milk, and she ATE EVERYTHING."

"She is better, she is better," said Straw, Clover, Noisy, Cotton, and all the others in turn, as they walked into the meadow.

All day, they talked so much, and all at one time, that no one knew what anyone else said.

It was Sunday when Veronica came out of her house.

All the animals saw her at the same time. They were *waiting* for her. "Here is Veronica!" they all cried at once.

They flew, galloped, ran, and danced around her, calling: "Good morning, Veronica, GOOD MORNING! GOOD MORNING! Welcome to our meadow."

"Good morning, my friends," said Veronica. And her smile was the biggest hippopotamus smile. *Very* big.

"What a lovely smile," said Noisy to Straw. "It shows how kind she is."

"You know," said Pig to Goat, "she has very sweet eyes, I think. Like a deer's."

"I don't mind at all if she muddies the pond," said Clover. "We muddy it too. A little."

"I feel the same way about the grass," said Straw. "What do I care if the grass is standing up or lying flat? It has the same taste."

"Don't you think HIPPOPOTAMUS is a pretty name?" Petunia asked Ida.

"I do," said Ida. "She *is* a pretty hippopotamus, too."

"Cock-a-doodle-doo," sang King from the top of Veronica's nose.
"She is *our* hippopotamus. Cock-a-doodle-doo!"

There was never such a gay Sunday on
Mr. Pumpkin's farm. Veronica said the farm was
even more beautiful than it seemed the first day
she came.

IT WAS INDEED JUST RIGHT